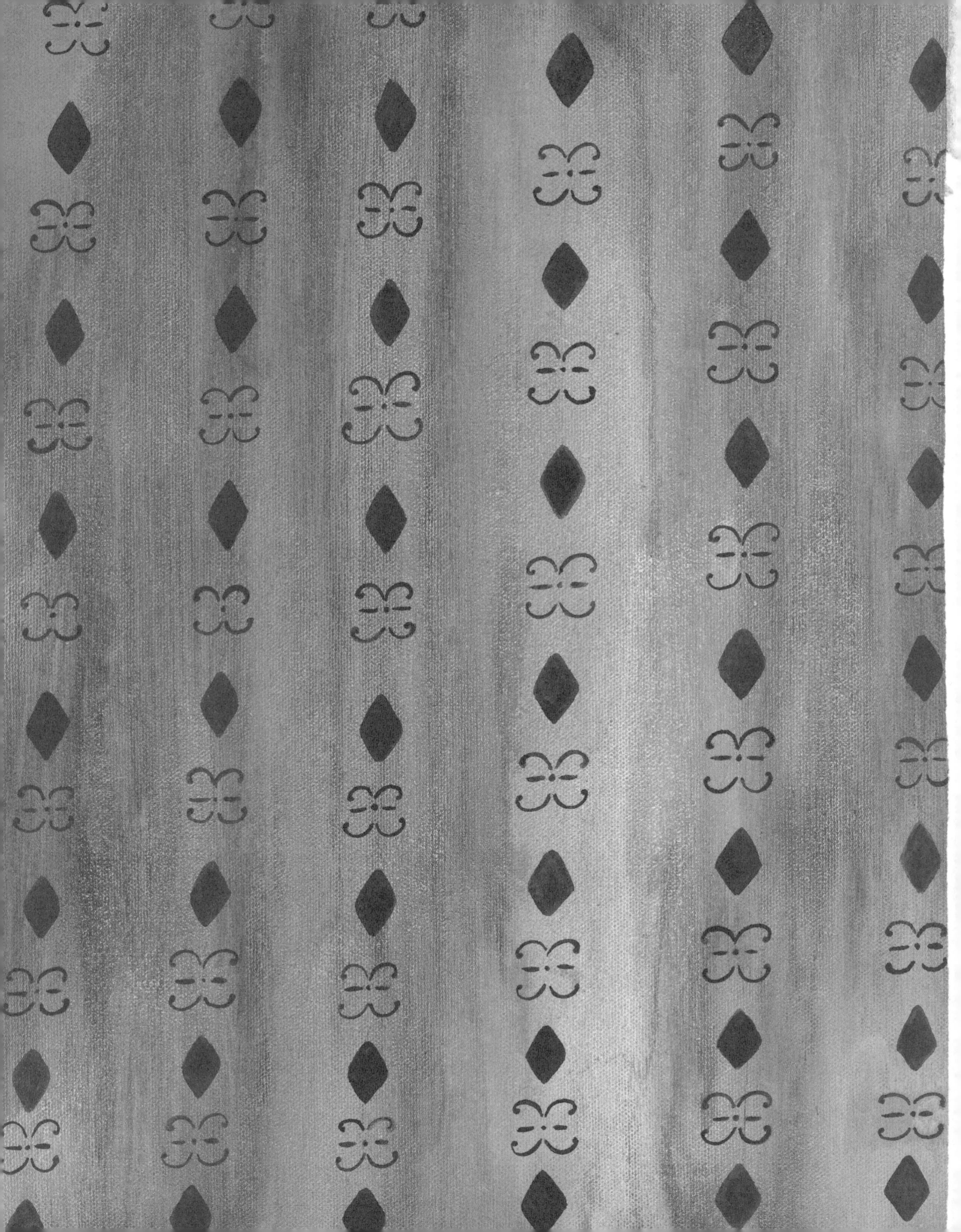

# Little Girl in a Red Dress with Cat and Dog

BY
NICHOLAS B. A. NICHOLSON

PAINTINGS BY
CYNTHIA VON BUHLER

VIKING

For my family, and to the memory of Alice Miller Bregman.

— N. B. A. N.

To my godchild, Dakota Lee O'Dell

—C. V. B.

ACKNOWLEDGMENTS

I would like to thank a number of people who have been helpful in the conception and completion of this book. I would like to thank Sara Clinton, Katherine Fukushima, and Rebecca Danziger, who all thought this was a good idea six years ago, when we served on the Junior committee of the Museum of American Folk Art. My thanks also for the kind support of Gerard C. Wertkin, director of the museum. I also thank for their help and good humor my former colleagues in the American Furniture and Decorative Arts department at Christie's: John Hays, Susan Kleckner, and Margot Rosenberg. Finally, my thanks and affection to my editor, Deborah Brodie, and my father/agent, George Nicholson, who both believed in this project from the beginning.

— N. B. A. N.

VIKING

Published by the Penguin Group

Penguin Putnam Inc., 375 Hudson Street, New York, New York 10014, U.S.A.

Penguin Books Ltd, Registered Offices: Harmondsworth, Middlesex, England

First published in 1998 by Viking, a division of Penguin Putnam Inc.

1 3 5 7 9 10 8 6 4 2



LIBRARY OF CONGRESS CATALOGING-IN-PUBLICATION DATA

Nicholson, Nicholas B. A.

Little girl in a red dress with cat and dog / by Nicholas B. A. Nicholson ; illustrated by Cynthia von Buhler.

p. cm.

Summary: Tells a fictionalized story of how this actual portrait of a young farm girl came to be painted by Ammi Phillips sometime around 1835 in Dutchess County, New York.

ISBN 0-670-87183-4

[1. Farm life—New York (State)—Fiction. 2. Family life—Fiction. 3. Portraits—Fiction. 4. Phillips, Ammi, 1788–1865—Fiction.] I. Buhler, Cynthia von, ill. II. Title.

PZ7.N5543Po 1998 [E]—dc21 96-45385 CIP AC

Manufactured in China Set in Opti Navel

The art was prepared with gouache on stretched linen canvas; sponging and layering the paint created the antique affect.

That's me over the fireplace.

hen I was a little girl and living with my parents on the farm near Amenia, New York, Mr. Ammi Phillips came, and I sat for a portrait. Well, I almost sat. In those days, I couldn't sit still for long.

I was always running. I had a large family then, and each of us had lots to do on our farm. Oh, we didn't work in the fields—we had hired workers to do that—but we all had plenty to do around the house.

My father sat in his office and paid workers and bills. But I was too young to understand. "You make too much noise running around the office, and you shuffle all my papers," said my father. "Go help your mother."

My mother ran the household and entertained the ladies who went to church with us. She served them tea in the parlor with the painted furniture we weren't allowed to touch. But I was too little to stay. "You'll only be underfoot while I serve the tea and pass the apple cake," said my mother. "Go help your brothers."

My brothers, Ezekiel and Benjamin and Joseph and Obadiah, cut wood. But it was too dangerous for me to help. "You'll slip and cut yourself, and besides, the logs are too heavy for you to lift," said my brothers. "Go help your sisters."

My sisters, Rebecca and Sarah and Esther, worked on their needlework, but it was too complicated for me to try. "You'll only knot the silks and tear the linen, and besides, your little fingers are too clumsy," said my sisters. "Go help Mrs. Tucker in the kitchen."

And in the kitchen, Mrs. Tucker cooked and baked. But she was too busy to pay any attention to me at all, or tell me to go anywhere.

So mostly I ran around with Cat and Dog. I looked out my little window shaped like a fan, waiting to grow up, or for something exciting to happen—whichever came first.

But then, on a warm spring night when the skies were thick with stars, I saw a stranger make his way up the winding road to our house, where candles gleamed in every window.

Mr. Ammi Phillips was a painter. He told my parents and me that he traveled around painting country folk, and he wanted to paint the three of us. I held my breath. A real painter!

"I will paint your whole family!" exclaimed Mr. Phillips, unpacking his paints and brushes and jars and bottles and canvas and wood. "And it won't be too expensive—I charge per person!" he said, smiling.

Just then, Ezekiel and Benjamin and Joseph and Obadiah and Rebecca and Sarah and Esther came in from the kitchen. "Oh, dear," my mother said. "Our whole family? Really?"

"I'm far too busy to sit for a portrait," said my father. "I have a farm to run."

"I'm too busy as well," said my mother. "I have to run the household and entertain the sodality."

“We have a lot of wood to chop, and we’re far too dirty,” said my brothers Ezekiel, Benjamin, Joseph, and Obadiah.

“And we are busy with our needlework,” said my sisters Sarah, Rebecca, and Esther to the painter, pulling out their pretty samplers.

"I'll do it!" I hollered. And everybody turned to look.

"Well, that settles it," said Mr. Phillips, smiling at me. "One painting, one girl, one fee."

My parents smiled and nodded.

"And Cat and Dog," I added. "They're not people, so you'll do them for free, won't you?" And everyone laughed.

The next day, Cat and Dog and I sat in the front parlor, where the light was best to see for painting. Mr. Phillips started painting my face. I hated it. I had to sit very still. "This is hard," I said.

"Painting is, too," agreed Mr. Phillips.

"Oh how darling she is!" all the ladies exclaimed to my mother. "How nice you look, my pretty pumpkin!" said my mother. And Mr. Phillips and I stayed and ate cherry tarts in the parlor with the ladies all afternoon. Suddenly, sitting still wasn't so very difficult after all.

The next day, we went outside and painted in the sun so Cat and Dog could be in the fresh air. "That looks like fun!" said my brothers, and they let me break the twigs off the logs all afternoon.

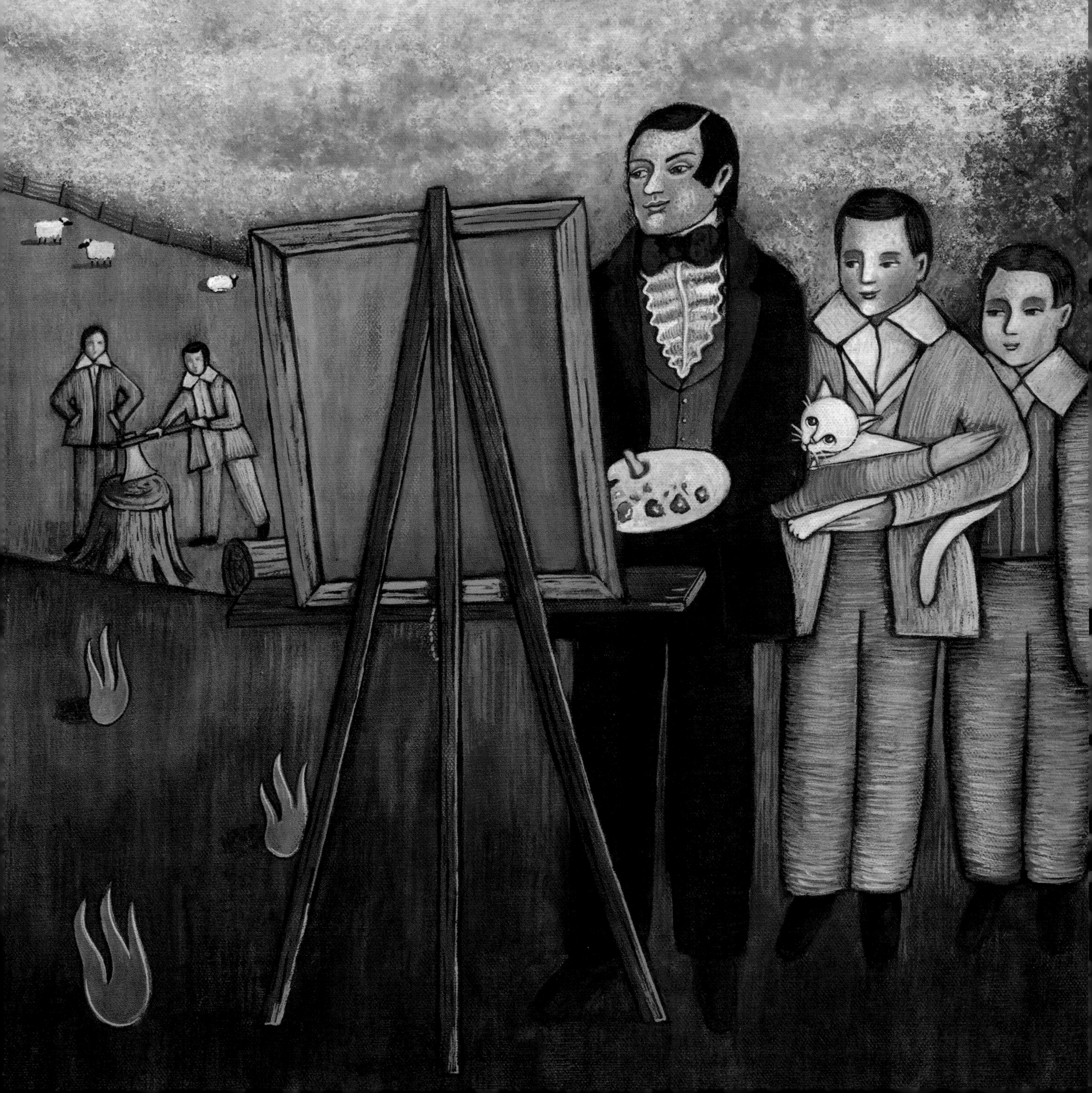

The day after that, my sisters came to watch. "You must wear my lace pantalettes!" said my sister Sarah.

"And you must wear my favorite red dress," said my sister Rebecca.

"And you must wear my coral beads, come all the way from the Caribbean on a trading ship," said my oldest sister, Esther.

And Mr. Phillips painted, and my sisters and I chattered. And do you know what? That afternoon, my sisters taught me to sew.

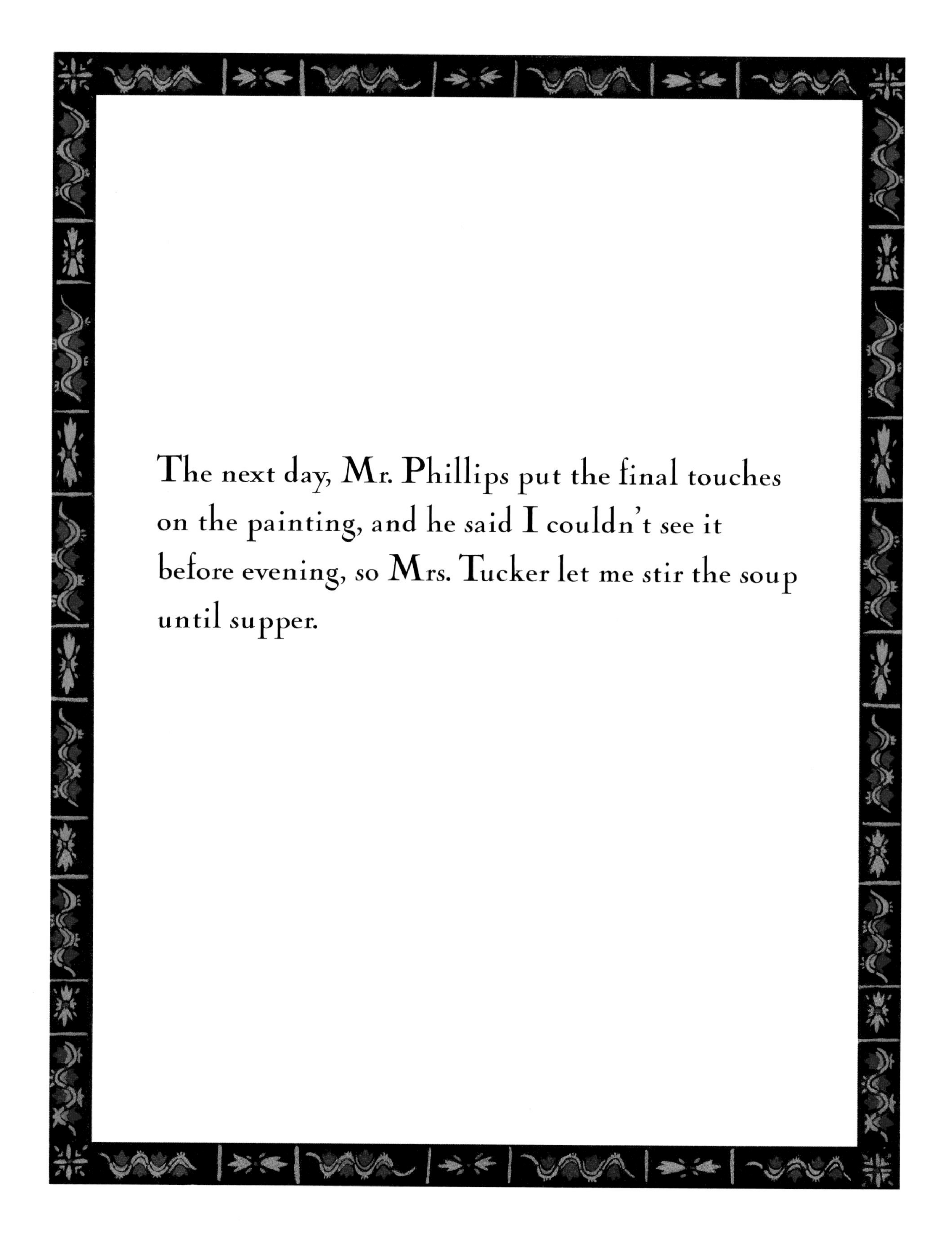

The next day, Mr. Phillips put the final touches on the painting, and he said I couldn't see it before evening, so Mrs. Tucker let me stir the soup until supper.

That night, when we came into the dining room, the painting of me and Cat and Dog was hanging over the fireplace. Everyone clapped their hands, and Dog

barked, and Cat purred, and my mother even cried a little. My father gave Mr. Phillips a purse full of silver coins, and then we all ate together.

I told Mr. Phillips that I would miss him very much, and after supper, he said good-bye and left.

Many years later I still think of Ammi Phillips. I found out that there are more portraits of little girls in red dresses like mine. But I like to think that's because Mr. Phillips missed me, too.

## A Note to Teachers and Parents

It is hard to believe that there was ever a time when Shaker furniture, Connecticut Valley School paintings, and even Philadelphia Chippendale furniture weren't considered precious historical objects, but there was. American folk art was generally held in low esteem until the 1920s, when the urge to save American historic buildings and material culture finally became part of the public consciousness, with collectors like industrialists E. I. DuPont and Henry Ford buying whole buildings and their contents. It was with the rise of these collections that we began to treat our American cultural heritage with respect.

The idea for this book came when I was working with the Junior Committee of the Museum of American Folk Art in New York City, where the definitive version of the painting by Ammi Phillips exists. The painting *Portrait of a Little Girl in a Red Dress with Cat and Dog* was done in an area near Amenia, New York, in about 1835. Ammi Phillips, a self-taught painter, traveled around northern New York, Connecticut, and Massachusetts, offering to paint the pictures of the farmers who lived in that area.

Life was hard for those early farmers, but by the 1830s the towns had grown larger, and the farms more profitable. Some of the farmers did well, allowing them to buy goods from other states, and even from Europe. One of the most desirable luxuries was artwork. Paintings were commissioned only for very special occasions: sometimes double portraits were painted for weddings; sometimes a painting included the whole family.

We know nothing of the girl in this portrait, but we do know that Ammi Phillips had been using the same composition repeatedly from about 1830. Several other versions of this painting exist in private American collections and in the Baltimore Museum of Art, the Art Museum of Princeton University, and the Terra Museum of American Art in Chicago. But the painting in New York speaks to us on a gut emotional level in a way the other versions do not—perhaps indicating a degree of personal attachment to the sitter that was not present in the other versions. It was that immediate response which triggered this book, and it is that sense which I hope children take away from it: that folk art forms an immediate personal relationship with its viewer, just as I believe Ammi Phillips did with his sitter.

— N. B. A. N.